I0633558

BOOTSIE'S WAR YEARS

A DARK LAUGHTER COLLECTION

by Ollie Harrington

Compilation and annotations by Nat Gertler

Foreword by Qiana Whitted

About Comics | Camarillo, California

Bootsie's War Years: a Dark Laughter collection

Cartoons copyright © Dr. Helma Harrington, Berlin. Used by permission.
Annotations and compilation copyright 2022 About Comics.
Foreword copyright 2022 Qiana Whitted.

ISBN-13: 978-1-949996-33-3

Continuous printing beginning January, 2022.

For wholesale orders, customized editions and other inquiries, email questions@aboutcomics.com

Foreword

Qiana Whitted

An illustration on the front page of the *Pittsburgh Courier* in February 1942 marked the start of the prominent Black newspaper's Double V Campaign. Printed without comment above the masthead, the image featured two beveled-edge Vs for "Double Victory" beneath the wings of an American eagle, the sun shining bright in the background. The World War II slogan in the drawing, which proclaimed "Democracy – At Home and Abroad," had been prompted by a letter printed previously from James G. Thompson, a defense worker from Wichita, Kansas.

In Thompson's letter to the *Courier* editors, he referenced the popular "V for Victory" war cry against totalitarian aggression and proposed a version that acknowledged the existential strivings of African Americans who were being asked to defend a country where racial segregation was legally sanctioned and violently enforced. "I suggest that while we keep defense and victory in the forefront that we don't lose sight of our fight for true democracy at home," Thompson wrote, before adding: "For surely those who perpetrate these ugly prejudices here are seeking to destroy our democratic form of government just as surely as the Axis forces."

The *Courier* registered public enthusiasm for the Double V Campaign through its reporting and commentary, as well as photographs of local readers, uniformed soldiers, and national celebrities signaling the twin Vs with their hands. Also documented were the Double V gardens, the special pageants, pins, songs, hairstyles, and clubs; Black Baptist churches held a "National Negro Double Victory Day" on Easter Sunday in 1942. All the while, illustrations continued to tout the campaign's efforts through original editorial artwork and even in the *Courier* comics section, where the distinct logo surfaced on several occasions in Wilbert L. Holloway's "Sunnyboy Sam" comic strip.

Yet the cartoons that comprise *Bootsie's War Years* in this collection by Ollie Harrington are among the most compelling visual chronicles of the views that fueled the Double V Campaign. The "Dark Laughter" series in which Bootsie first appeared had been in circulation since the Depression and as a result, according to M. Thomas Inge, Bootsie was "the first black newspaper comic character to achieve a national reputation." In contrast to Holloway's comic, direct references to the Double V Campaign did not appear in Harrington's accounts of Bootsie's exploits. Instead, the New York-born cartoonist satirized the stakes of the war effort for Bootsie and his neighbors through their daily interactions in the tenement hallways, diners, and sidewalks of Harlem.

From week to week, the one-panel gag cartoons centered Brother Bootsie as the main source of conflict (whether he was physically present or not). Harrington was adept at generating comic relief through illustrations of the frenzied fallout: men with bandaged heads surveyed the aftermath of Bootsie's poker night in the busted furniture around them, women in jaunty hats whispered disapprovingly about his antics over morning coffee. Harrington's loose and expressive artistic style was well suited for capturing the stunned reactions of those who had witnessed Bootsie's foolhardy schemes to impress a date, to enjoy a free meal, or to cover next month's rent.

Bootsie is also pictured amid the absurdity as an American struggling to grasp where he and his community stand in relation to the war's theater of operations in Europe. The cartoons show Bootsie attempting to elude the draft board and botching his duties as an air-raid warden, while the latest political maneuvers in Washington (along with gas rationing) spark heated debate among his friends at the lodge. Over time, Bootsie's encounters generate a different kind of visual rhetoric that makes plain the unspoken contradictions of wartime sacrifice for working-class African Americans. One cartoon captures Bootsie in conversation with a man who appears to be seated in the back alley of an apartment building, surrounded by trash and with his shoes split open to reveal his toes. The man gestures ironically to the scene around him and says: "Well jest tell me this Bootsie – how tha devil can Hitler whup us with all our great wealth" (November 8, 1941). What does the call to serve mean for people whose aspirations are thwarted as a matter of course and whose lives are treated as if they are expendable in their own country?

At the same time, Bootsie's reluctance to take part in the war effort is confounded by an ambition to earn the respect of his family and friends. Harrington demonstrates that, behind the slogans and symbols, pride takes shape in complicated ways and can be reciprocated unexpectedly. Once Bootsie has enlisted, for instance, a poignant episode finds him at the train station surrounded by an intimate circle of Black men, women, and a child. In the center, an older woman opens her arms wide to him and declares: "Bootsie, you're a dirty, low-down, no-good scoundrel. You ain't nothin' and you ain't never gonna be nothin'… but if you don't come back to us I don't know what we gonna do" (February 17, 1945).

Not surprisingly, Private Bootsie brings the world with him to the front. He runs into old enemies during combat training (November 13, 1943), teaches new friends his New York card tricks (February 24, 1945), and is reminded, as he heads into battle, that he still owes a buddy five dollars (April 28, 1945). On more sobering occasions, Harrington drew on his experience as a war correspondent to reflect on the seemingly minor social differences overseas that would have had tremendous implications for African Americans, such as when Bootsie is pictured riding in a horse-drawn carriage. A fellow soldier observes: "This shore ain't Mississippi, is it Bootsie?" (June 16, 1945). The two men glance not at their surroundings, but at each other with a look of recognition and a contemplative smile while readers supply the sounds of the turning wheels and the horse quietly trotting in the background.

Bootsie and other Black veterans would eventually return to places like Mississippi where racial terrorism formed a Blitzkrieg of its own. The spike in violence after World War II was not limited to the South, of course, and had consequences nationwide. So much so that Bootsie is pictured in one cartoon carrying a violin case around town – presumably to hide a weapon -- after reading in the *Courier* about "them four folks getting lynched in Georgia" (August 3, 1946). While in another conversation, there is a rumor that news of a lynching has Bootsie in his room making an atomic bomb (August 24, 1946).

Ironically enough, both examples allude to the tools and techniques that Bootsie would have acquired in defense of his country, and that effectively illustrate the frustrations broached by Thompson in his 1942 *Courier* letter: "Should I sacrifice my life to live half American? Will things be better for the next generation in the peace to follow? Would it be demanding too much to demand full citizenship rights in exchange for the sacrificing of my life?" Ultimately, such demands are at the heart of the irreverent humor and shrewd observations of Bootsie's everyday encounters – the right to live as an American and to matter *fully* as a human being. *Bootsie's War Years* is an important archive of this effort. As the Black press called for a deeper reckoning on the home front during World War II, one prompted by hopes of a Double Victory, Harrington used his space on the comics page to show his beloved character working through the same crucial questions about race and the realities of freedom, democracy, and citizenship in his own unique way.

◆ ◇ ◆ ◇ ◆ ◇ ◆

Qiana Whitted *is professor of English and African American Studies at the University of South Carolina. She is the author of the Eisner Award-winning book,* EC Comics: Race, Shock, and Social Protest *and editor of* Inks: The Journal of the Comics Studies Society.

Compiler's Notes

It is said that a man who has a watch always knows what time it is, but the man who has two watches is never quite sure.

Ollie Harrington's comic panel "Dark Laughter" first appeared in the New York-based *Amsterdam News* in May of 1935, and the character of Bootsie made his first appearance in the series in the final week of that year. By 1941, when the cartoons in this book start, the strip was being syndicated to Black weeklies across the United States. This creates a problems with putting specific dates on these cartoons. The most obvious difficulty comes from the various weeklies not publishing on the same day of the week. Even allowing for that, the fact that the newspapers didn't always publish the cartoons in the same order makes it hard to put an official date on anything. The cartoons reproduced here were taken from the archives of several different papers. For panels before 1944, the date listed on each page is *a* date that that panel appeared in *a* paper (generally, the paper we've used as the source for that cartoon.)

That situation simplifies after Harrington's one-year break from the cartoon to serve as a war correspondent. Upon his return in 1945 the strip was no longer syndicated, but ran exclusively in the *Pittsburgh Courier*. (Despite the paper's name, the *Courier* was a national paper, with localized editions produced in various markets.) This gives us a single date for these cartoons.

The dates often seem far apart. "Dark Laughter" sometimes simply didn't appear in a given a week. At other times, Harrington would provide a previously-drawn cartoon, often with a new caption. In cases where the image was reused with a substantially different joke, we've included a mention of that alternate caption where the art first appears. Otherwise, we just skipped it.

"Brother Bootsie, kind'a clean up aroun' here for me an'
Stewmeat, will ya? We been up all night tryin' to figger out this
war sityation."

"Well no we aint gonna take on Joe Louis but soon's he retires we're gonna start campaignin'."

This panel originally ran in May 1941. When heavyweight champion Joe Louis enlisted in the Army in January 1942, it inspired a March 1942 reuse of the art with the new caption, "Well since Joe's fightin' for the army now, Me and Boots figgered we'd hold things down out here 'till he comes back."

May 8, 1941

"He just keeps ridin' up and down this street 'cause he don't like you an' me."

"There goes brother Bootsie. He's got to go down to his draft board for a physical examination."

This May 1941 art was reused in August of the following year, with the caption "Well, Bootsie may have been hurt in that accident, but I know he was to report to his draft board."

May 22, 1941

"Doc, I brought my friend Bootsie aroun'. He wants to know if you can give him a case of T.B. before they calls his number."

The US Army started their screening of potential draftees for tuberculosis (T.B.) during World War I. While a vaccine had been invented in the 1920s, the disease was still killing about 60,000 Americans per year in 1941. The art, which is already recycled in this May 1941 appearance, was reused in February 1943 with the caption "My friend Bootsie dreamed he was a captain. He wants to be examined to find out if there is anything wrong."

"The boys was enjoyin' themselves fine—when Brother Bootsie
ask somebody who was goin' to win the war."

This art was reused in February 1942, with the caption "The boy was quiet
an' everything. Then somebody whispered in Bootsie's ear that there was
an air raid—"

June 7, 1941

"Brother Bootsie there's a couple of gents out here with a note
for you – an' I guess you better bring your hat an' coat with you"

"Whatyasay Boots, we heard 'bout you gittin' your questionairre
so we came on over to look over your togs."

This July 1941 panel was reused in July 1946, with the caption "What do you
say, Bootsie? We heard you got messed up an' wuz over at the horsepital, so
we figgered you wouldn't be needing these duds for a while."

June 21, 1941

"Now don't get excited Honey it was a accident. Bootsie was just explainin' a air-raid"

The art from this June 1941 panel was reused in June of 1946 with a new caption — "It ain't nothin' at all, Baby Doll... Bootsie wuz jest kind'a explainin' whut he'd a done if HE had been down there in Columbia, Tennessee." — reflecting a race riot that had taken place in February of that year.

"But Baby, I had to buy him a drape like that. After all he's my son too an' when he falls out with me he's got to fall out right."

It was Malcolm X — then known as Detroit Red — who referred to a zoot suit as a "killer-diller coat with a drape shape, reet-pleats, and shoulders padded like a lunatic's cell."

July 3, 1941

"Doggone! We gonna have to take Bootsie off that scaffold.
Every day when that lunch whistle blows he does
the same thing."

"That settles it, I'm gonna let y'all stay dumb. I also gonna bring up no more war discussions. I'm gonna keep all that inside stuff to myself."

When this art was reused in September 1942, it was with a caption that no longer invoked the war: "I don't care. I still think my argument was correct."

"Oh-Er—Hullo Baby, Uh—I didn't expect you out here at the camp today. The General just asked me to kind'a instruct some of these rookies on how to peel potatoes."

"Thanks for the movies an' a very swell evenin' Mr. Bootsie—
But I really don't want to discuss no war or politics or nothin'."

July 31, 1941

"Every time Bootsie an' Stewmeat comes to get a gallon of gas
for their new Cadillac they disagree about who bought the
gallon the last time."

"The way I figgers it Bootsie, the members is gettin' a little older
and more settled down. Why not a soul got throwed overboard
during the whole excursion."

"Don't forget to duck back there Bootsie, some of these branches are kind'a low."

"Well Bootsie, jest as soon as you release my old lady, I want you to look into yo crystal ball and tell me whut I got in my pocket an' whut is I gonna do with it."

September 4, 1941

"It fits jes' like a glove brother Bootsie—an' it's the very same number I made up for Clark Gable—Of course Gable can't let folks know that."

"Oh brother dear, I want you to meet Mr. Bootsie, the gent I was telling you about, who said he could get me a job singin' with any of the big bands."

"Them chicks are as sharp as a tack, Boots, but dig the lunch box them beat chicks got over there."

"Baby, I Don't Want to Set the World on Fire"

When this October 1941 panel reran ten months later, it no longer had a reference to the Ink Spots hit "I Don't Want to Set the World on Fire." Instead, the caption read "I was just wondering what makes a fellow rush out and eat and then remember he forgot his wallet."

October 18, 1941

"An' this is little Pluto's room—He is jest a little angel."

"I guess we over-practiced – We ain't got no men left to play the real game."

October 30, 1941

"I borrowed him from my sister-in-law. I gotta date with Mr. Bootsie tonight and thought I oughta have him around."

"That elevator boy looks just like Major Bootsie, the officer we met last nite who said he was in the Air Corps."

November 6, 1941

"Well jest tell me this Bootsie—how tha devil can Hitler whup us with all our great wealth."

"Of course, Brother Bootsie, me an' the old lady would love to
have you stay for dinner –that is, if you wants to."

November 29, 1941

"You big baboon. You think you can make me quit you don'cha?
Well I ain't see—not 'til after Christmas."

"Now you is a military man, ain't ya? We'l, me and Bootsie wants some information. How many tanks, guns and planes do ya figger we need to supply ya with to beat Hitler?"

December 13, 1941

"Mister Bootsie was tellin' me that he was goin' to buy it, but they wanted him to pay seven dollars an' fifty cents more than he thought it was worth."

In 1943, with wartime purchasing restrictions on, this panel was reprinted with the caption "Bootsie said last night he was gonna get me a car like this, if it hadn't been for gas rationing."

December 20, 1941

"Mr. Bootsie, I thought we wuz gonna get in trouble when you
said dat stop signal was jus' Communist propaganda."

December 25, 1941

"Now, Pluto, you stop beatin' your Uncle Bootsie with the
present he give you. Go outside an' beat somebody who ain't
give you nothin'."

"I'm getting scared as h - —They may lower the draft age again."

This image reran in 1943 with the caption "Uncle Bootsie told me to start yellin' if the man doesn't give him credit."

January 3, 1942

"Guess we better not leave the tree up too long, the landlord might think we got somethin' an' jack the rent up."

"Say Bootsie Old Man, where did you say you got them tickets?"

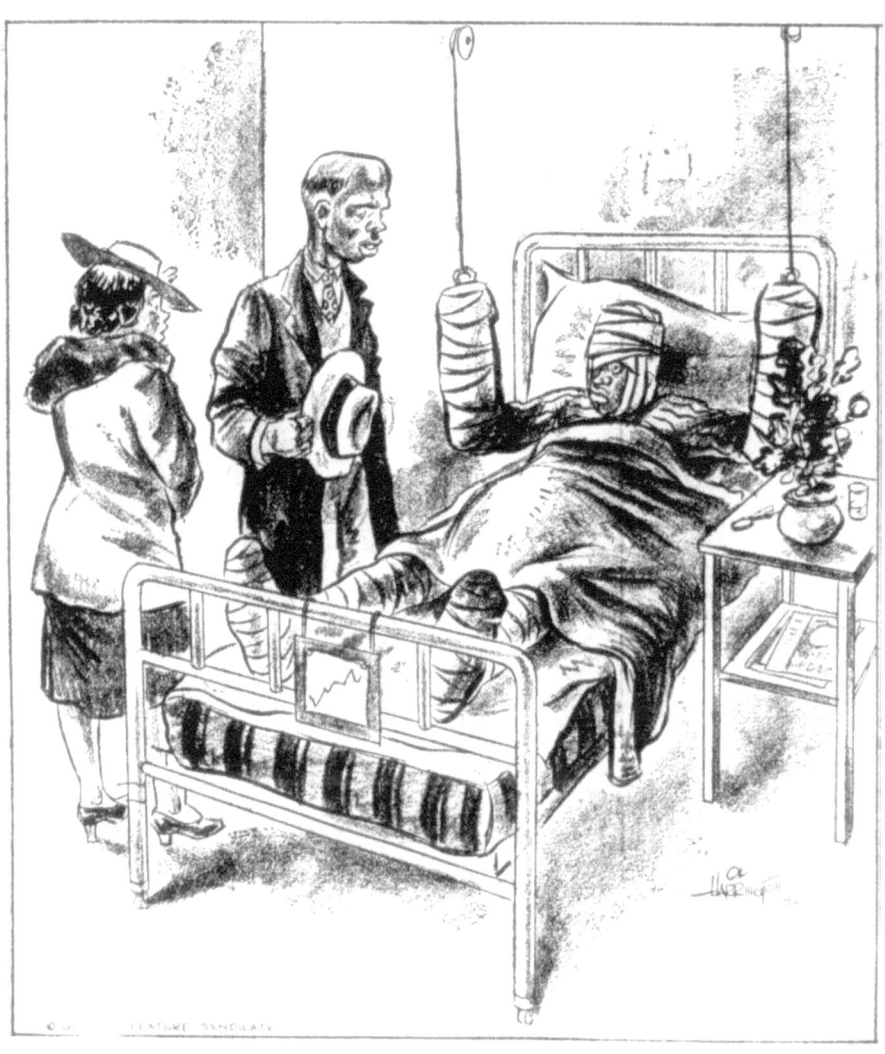

"Well no Brother Ferguson, it wus'nt no real air raid; it was just a practice one but Bootsie got a little excited."

"Bootsie there is awful worried. He read there the gov'ts gonna
charge every man, woman, and child fo' hundred bucks for the
war effort, an' he ain't had his hands on ten dollars in the
last five years."

January 31, 1942

"Well, with everything so expensive these days I've got to get rid of Bootsie or the dog— and you know I couldn't be so cruel to the dog."

"An' don't even bother me no more—I don't want nothin' the army turned down. My requirements is higher than anybody's army."

Usually when Harrrington reused an image, he did nothing more to it than touch-up the date. In this case, however, he's taken an image that appeared in December 1941 and added a third person to the cartoon.

February 14, 1942

"Not so fast, Mr. Bootsie. Now you say you can get a job in the national defense. But, well why ain't you got one for yourself."

"You see, Mr. Bootsie, the cost of livin' has gone up so high that I had to refinance your room. So from now on, yo' time to sleep in yo' bed is on Shift 2B."

"Now look here, Bootsie. You wolf, I don't care if the gov't does want you to save on tires. Wait 'til you get out'a these woods before you start sav'in 'em."

"How come you always waits 'til you get to the ticket office
before you remembers you forgot your wallet."

April 11, 1942

"Patriotic or no patriotic, I told you I want you to make that guy stop making faces at me."

"Bootsie said he was gonna tell his landlady that the government frozed rents 'til after the war."

September 3, 1942

"Please tell our good friend Bootsie to step to the door. There is a little matter of a check that he gave us that we want to adjust."

"Bootsie just won't work... Sayas he's plannin on taking a big job; so he's restin' up."

October 1, 1942

"Mr. Brown, did the board tell a gent named Bootsie to prove
that he has dependents? Well, he's got 'em here now."

"I know you are hidin' in there Bootsie an' I know you been sneaken food in. That's gonna cost you fifty cents–fer privileges."

This image was reused in late 1945 with the caption "Now Mr. Bootsie, you don't have to hide under there just 'cause rent's due today. After all, you is a vet-ran."

October 22 1942

"It's your own fault. I keep tellin' you to stop kiddin' Bootsie about his draft board."

Is you-all from Harlem? You know a big shot over there named
Bootsie?

This image was reused in September 1945 with the caption "Now if
Bootsie an' them other cats went an' lost their heads just 'cause them
English chicks got all excited, y'all better hep 'em before they gets out
here."

December 12, 1942

"Now look here, Bootsie. You ain't gonna quit me this year just
'fore Christmas, like you did last year?"

"Bootsie your health is fine. But I can see a pair of aces coming into your life."

The ante was upped when this art was reused in 1946 with the new caption "Man, I can't undertan' what this crystal is tryin' to put down. All I can see in it is MY wife!"

January 16, 1943

"Well, Bootsie, I wouldn't mind lending you five bucks but you
is too much of a risk. I mean your social life."

"Well, Bootsie, we ain't exactly callin' you no liar—but why should the Gov'ment ask you for advice when they got all them generals an' things right there in Wash'nun?"

February 27, 1943

"So this feller said that for fifty bucks he could fix me right up at the draft board… so I gave him fifty bucks…"

"Pore Brother Butts... just look at 'im. He ain't been right since he got in the way of that Air Raid Warden, Bootsie, who thought it was a real air raid."

March 13, 1943

"Sumpin tells me Bootsie aint gonna like this!"

"Hello, Bootsie—Remember that hot tip you gave me? Well come on down here. I want to thank you for it personal."

April 10, 1943

"I'd like to take a course in commando tactics. You see, I goes with a feller named Bootsie."

"We picked him up as a mugger suspect—now we want the charge changed to resisting arrest, battery and assault, attempted murder and disorderly conduct."

April 24, 1943

"Now Mr. Bootsie we ain't that dumb. If you was in that raid on Tokyo, why wasn't your picture in the papers with Jimmy Doolittle?"

Lieutenant Colonel James Doolittle led an air raid on Tokyo and other areas of Japan on April 18, 1942, as retaliation to the bombing of Pearl Harbor four months earlier.

"Mr. Bootsie, How you gonna teach me to ride this bicycle if you keep on doin' that?"

May 15, 1943

"Well, I went to this fine function with Bootsie…. He said that they were his boys an' that he had everything under control.

"Mister Bootsie, thanks for the night club an' the dinner an' ev'rything but ain't no use in oversportin' yourself.... In other words, it's time for you to leave."

May 29, 1943

"Mr. Bootsie, do you realize that them sailors are whistlin' at me…. What are you goin' to do about it?"

"Brother Bootsie's feelin' awful bad on account of the new tax bill. He only made ten bucks las' year so the government ain't had no tax to forgive him for anyway."

"There's a gent here named Mr. Bootsie…. He say we sent a card
for him to come in an' take his physicals."

"I figgered we better call the poker game off, Boots. The old
lady's in the mood to hurt somebody."

"Not so fast—Mr. Bootsie, I said when you get a job—not when you think about getting one."

"Mr. Bootsie, this is my baby brother…. He is goin' up with us to your apartment to get them ration stamps you promised me."

"I know just whut you're thinkin' Bootsie. But I saw her pull a feller in yestid'y…. After she had done knocked the h..l out of him."

"Bootsie, you old wolf... an' anyway, I don't need no gas ration
stamps. I ain't got no car."

August 28, 1943

"Well, I kept tellin' you when you hear them air-raid whistles blow, don't stand in front of that house Mr. Bootsie comes out of!"

"You see there, Mr. Jones…. I told you about lettin' Mr. Bootsie's social and athletic club meet up in his room."

September 25, 1943

"It ain't nobody but Mr. Bootsie…. Lots of 'em acts like that
when I hand 'em that long envelope."

**The letter in the "long envelope" brought you greetings from the
President and then let you know that you had been drafted.**

"Why, no, we hadn't done nothing to Bootsie. We heard Uncle had done sent for him an' we jes' went over to pay our respects, that's all!"

The "Uncle" here is Uncle Sam, a nickname for the US government.

October 23, 1943

"Bootsie, you liable to come out of the Army a great hero…
Even if you don't the lodge can put up a great big memorial. So
why worry?"

October 30, 1943

"Goodbye Bootsie Baby… An' don't fergit, send me back a
Japanese an' a Nazi… an' a Flyin' Fortress!"

The Boeing B-17 Flying Fortress was a bomber manufactured from 1936
through 1945. A year before this cartoon ran, the Warner Bros movie
Flying Fortress depicted a B-17 bombing of Berlin, Germany.

November 6, 1943

"Well, well, well, who used to get me whipped about the head every Sat'd'y night?"

"Say, Bootsie, when you reaches the end of this floor, deliver this letter to the mess sergeant. I wuz gonna mail it but you may get there before the mail officer!"

December 11, 1943

"O.K., Private Bootsie, two more guesses… what's the best way
to get OVER an obstacle?"

Bootsie disappeared from the comics pages for all of 1944 as cartoonist Ollie Harrington took on another role: war correspondent.

SATURDAY, JUNE 17, 1944

99th Head Lauds Courier Writer

FAIRMONT, W. Va.—In speaking of the correspondents representing Negro newspapers in war zones whom he had met during his stay overseas, Major George Spencer Roberts, commanding officer of the 99th Pursuit Squadron, was particularly loud in his praise of The Courier's Ol Harrington, now in Italy.

"Harrington is doing a job that we all feel is important. He is covering the activities of the G-I's and not the 'glamour boys,' as we have come to call ourselves (he was referring to the Negro fliers in that area). The folks back home are wont to forget that those men on the ground are doing as important a job as we up there in the air. Harrington, in his stories, isn't letting them forget it."

———VV———

"Bootsie, you're a dirty, low-down, no-good scoundrel. You ain't nothin' and you ain't never gonna be nothin'… but if you don't come back to us I don't know what we gonna do."

"Well, things is usually quiet here but that new feller, Private Bootsie, wuz showin' the fellows one of them New York card games last night."

February 24, 1945

"…An' I, as Grand Master, serves notice on the Nazis an'
Japanese, on land, on sea, an' in the air, if dear Brother Bootsie
don't return, beware the wrath of the Social Dukes Benevolent
an' Athletic Association!"

March 3, 1945

"That's Bootsie all right, but he ain't under arrest. Them's the two cats he hired to be his bodyguard after he won all that cash in the game last night."

March 10, 1945

"Well, Bootsie, didn't you see the Colonel standin' behind you
when you called him all them names?"

"Here comes that damn sarjint agin. He never used to ride that nag so much 'til they put him on this clean-up detail."

March 24, 1945

"Say, Bootsie, didn't them friends of yours on your draft board send as assistant to carry your luggage?"

"Bootsie, you'd never guess it, but this sharp cat in the killin' drape was me… three Easters ago!"

April 7, 1945

"That's Bootsie's slit trench there… it's so deep he sprained both ankles jumpin' in it… Now he's at the Dressin' Station squawkin' for a Purple Heart."

The Purple Heart is a decoration given to US military members who are wounded or killed while serving.

"Bootsie just got a letter from his draft board. They want him to report for induction."

April 21, 1945

"Now, Bootsie, old man, be careful an' dont take chances. Remember you still owe me five bucks from las' payday."

"Look, Bootsie… that gives me a idea for that fine joint we're gonna open when we gits back home. We can have pretty colors like that right behind the bar!"

May 5, 1945

"Now, Bootsie, read that there manual careful... Do it say it's O.K. to call the Captain an' the Lootenant lousey... soon as the Armistice is declared?"

"Whenever I go out with brown Americanos there are so many meelitary poleece. Thees ees a great complimento to the brown Americanos, yes?"

May 19, 1945

"Well, hell, Bootsie, you should'a knowed the Colonel wuz gonna check up after he ask you to figure out your points."

Just after Germany ceded the war in March of 1945, the Army declared a points system for deciding when individual soldiers would return to the States. The system gave points for months of military service, more points for those months which had been spent overseas, and for the number of dependent children a soldier had.

"I'm awful sorry, Baby, but we ain't got nobody here by the name of COLONEL Bootsie. An' even if we did, he couldn't hire no secretary!"

June 2, 1945

"Bootsie, the Captain turned down our requeses for tha Purple Heart. Said Uncle Sam don't recernize wounds received in poker games an' sech."

"This shore ain't Mississippi, is it Bootsie?"

June 16, 1945

"Hold tight in that back seat, Bootsie, old man, here comes
another turn like that las' one!"

"It's that Damned Bootsie… He's learned to lie in Eyetalian!"

June 30, 1945

"Well, Captain, you know you got to keep an eye on these here civilians, so me an' Bootsie has been investigatin' some of the farms 'roun' here."

"Bootsie, I saw in the papers where on of them big-shot Senators said the boys wuz failures... I'm shore glad them guys can't read no more papers."

On June 29, 1945, during a filibuster against the forming of an anti-discrimination committee, Senator James Eastland (D-Mississippi) stated "The Negro soldier has been an utter and abysmal failure. I'm not saying that out of prejudice. That is what the responsible generals told us."

"Well, Bootsie, I guess we don't have to wory no more 'bout how many points we got."

"I heard confidential, the Colonel is going to have a litter of puppies in the morning."

July 28, 1945

"Signor Bootsie, eef you can give me the beeg job een Hollywood, you must be a great beeg man een America."

"Bootsie, this opera jive is solid. Now if they jes' had The Duke, Satchmo, Lionel, an' the Ink Spots to help out that Eyetalian band, it would be a killer."

The cited musicians would be pianist Edward "Duke" Ellington, trumpeter Louis Armstrong, vibraphonist Lionel Hampton, and the popular jazz vocalist group The Ink Spots.

August 11, 1945

"Bootsie, the folks back home will blow they tops when they sees this shot... Tha only thing missin' is a atom bomb."

"Ev'rybody else is talkin' about reconversion, so I guess I better
do some thinkin' about it myself."

After the American economy had very successfully turned
toward military production for World War II, it was faced with
the difficulties of "reconversion" — restoring an economy
focused on consumer purchases.

"They must'a got Old Bootsie's laundry mixed up with the Wac's."

The Women's Army Corps (originally the Women's Army Auxiliary Corps) was the female branch of the US Army from 1942 until gender desegregation of the Army in 1978. Individual members of the Corps were called WACs.

"Awright, Bootsie, don't start shovin'. I didn't see you shovin' to get up that gangplank when we wuz comin' over here."

"Remember, you can't say that to the chicks back home. First you got to say 'Glad to make your acquaintance... how ya been?'"

"The Gen'rul was gonna decorate some Joe named Bootsie—
two millionth man down the plank—but this Joe thinks the
Gen'rul is a MP or cop… so he flattens 'im!"

October 6, 1945

"Oh Lord, the house gonna git a bad name agin. I'm gonna have
to keep the ice box locked up all the time, an' ev'ybody's gonna
git all messed up… but jes' the same, we're sure glad you got
back."

"But, Mr. Bootsie, if you done all that by yourself, whut did they
need the whole U.S. Army for?"

October 20, 1945

"In our West Coast store we sold the mate to that suit
to Clark Gable."

"They say it started out to be a welcome-home party for one of them GI fellers named Bootsie... But it musta got outa hand or sumthin'."

November 3, 1945

"Now Mr. Bootsie, I don't want to know nothin' about you grabs
hold of the enemy… I already seen it in the movies."

"Now Mr. Bootsie, I know the Gov'ment wants us to go all out for the returned vet'rins an' all that… But after all, we only met this afternoon."

November 17, 1945

"It's the firs' time mummer's got us a turkey since the dooration an' they went an' invited Mister Bootsie to eat with us—you know that's just solid murder."

"An' now I presents our gues' of honor… Mister Bootsie, who's gonna tell 'bout them battles he wuz in… musical backgroun' by Tap Johnson an' his Frantic Wildcats."

December 8, 1945

"Well, I keep tellin' the chairman not to let Bootsie take the floor when we're havin' social matters under discussion."

December 22, 1945

"Mister Bootsie, it's twelve o'clock. Happy Noo Year. Do you know what folks is supposed to do at twelve o'clock Noo Years?"

"It's Bootsie an' his landlady agin… seems like he mentioned sump'n about a price ceilin' on room rents."

The federal government set price controls on a broad range of items, including rent, during the war years, and they remained in place for a while after. Even when President Truman ended most price ceilings ten months after this January 1946 cartoon, he left them in place for three things: sugar, rice, and dwelling rentals.

January 5, 1946

"Luther, bring me a broomstick or somethin'… 27-B says he
don't want to be bothered for rent'… Says he's busy writin' to the
President about some kind of fireside chat!"

"Well, I went over to this fine function with Bootsie… he said they was all his boys an' that he had everything under control."

January 26, 1946

"Now I ain't got time to fool aroun' Bootsie… Now what do you
want in the way of FOOD?"

"Bootsie shore wuzn't lyin'. The Gallup Poll sent him this letter wantin' to know whut does he think about worl' security and the atom bomb."

February 9, 1946

"Bootsie, ev'ry time I see a picture like that there 'Desire,' I begins to think a girl's got to be a solid fool to think that there's a future in you."

"Brother Bootsie, glad to see you servicemens at the services…
Guess it wuz them war experiences brought y'all back into the
flock."

February 23, 1946

"Bootsie, I'm tired of you comin' here askin' me whut's in the
ice-box. You ain't never said nothin' about us goin' out to a
restaurant if there ain't nothin' in the ice-box."

"I gotta put Bootsie an' them other overseas cats down… man, soon as you discusses cash with 'em they starts talkin' French an' Eyetalian and stuff."

March 23, 1946

"You mean Brother Bootsie came right out in the open an' said that?… Humph… the Army didn't change him none… He always was partial to spring."

"Now, Bootsie, keep your knees in an' your heels down an' there jest ain't no way in the world you can fall off."

April 20, 1946

"Say, Chief, for gawd's sake, look see if Bootsie's trapped in there, will ya?… he's got on my best drape he borrered yestidy."

"Now look, Mister Bootsie, the managemint's gittin' tired of you complainin' 'bout the meat bein' bad. Why dontcha put a lotta hot sauce on it like ev'ry body else."

May 4, 1946

"Well, I knows Brother Bootsie is a gent'man an' all that, but he did sneak out'a here this mornin' an' this is rent day… So I'm gonna sit in this door 'til he come home… Then he'll have to be a gent'man."

"Bootsie, you got a nerve bein' perticular about that suit... Why, there's folks would give a empire, kings would give their queens... jest to git of a suit like that!"

May 18, 1946

"Now wait, Mr. Bootsie! Before you say you can't afford it, let me ask you just one question… How many of your girls is workin' steady?"

"Mister Sweetbread, ain't that a shame?… that Boostie ain't satisfied to put 'em on hisself… He's even got to put pegged trousers on that pore dog."

July 20, 1946

"Look, Bootsie, you're my boy an' we didn't used to mind when you accidentally dropped around ev'ry day when we wuz havin' dinner… but there ain't no OPA now and it's gittin' too rough!"

The federal Office of Price Administration (OPA) which set price controls during the war was shut down in June of 1946 but was reinstated the next month, the month that this cartoon ran. It was, however, in the midst of political struggles that weakened it, and the office closed the following May.

"Ever since Bootsie read in The Courier 'bout that feller who got his eyes gouged out an' them four folks getting lynched in Georgia he's been carryin' that violin case aroun'. I didn't know he wuz musical."

In February 1946, on the day of his discharge from the Army, Sgt. Isaac Woodard Jr. was pulled from a bus by Batesburg, South Carolina police, beaten, then arrested for disorderly conduct. That night, Sheriff Lynwood Shull beat him into a state of permanent blindness. After this cartoon ran, Shull was cleared of all charges by an all white jury.

Two married Black couples — George W. and Mae Murray Dorsey, and Roger and Dorothy Malcom — were murdered by a gang of white men on July 25, 1946, with about 60 gunshots in Georgia, roughly sixty miles from Atlanta. No one was ever charged with their deaths.

August 3, 1946

"The situation down here with them crackers must be gittin' tough... Bootsie come in here an' just reads tha papers... He ain't made a pass at a waitress in two weeks."

"Yes, I'll go out on another date with ya, Mister Bootsie, long as you promise not to git frantic… You ought to stop tryin' to make his'try."

August 17, 1946

"Well, ever since all them folks been lynched, the kids tells me
Bootsie's been makin' a atomic bomb in his room… I kind'a
thought you ought to go up an' talk with him!"

August 24, 1946

"Bootsie, the cat who told you this wuz a used car should be locked up... Man, this car has been battered and assaulted with intent to kill!"

August 31, 1946

"Aw, Bootsie, I didn't mind gittin' throwed off the boatride, but
they should'a had more sense than to throw me off wid my
newes' drape on!"

September 7, 1946

Works Referenced for the Foreword:

Dolinar, Brian. "Humor Can Often Make Dents Where Sawed-Off Billiard Sticks Can't: The Bootsie Cartoons by Ollie Harrington." *Studies in American Humor* 3.14 (2006): 73-90

Thompson, James G. Letter to editor. *Pittsburgh Courier*, Jan. 31, 1942, 3.

Goldberg, Dan C. "During World War II, the black press campaigned for a double victory – over tyranny abroad and segregation at home," *The Undefeated*, May 25, 2020. https://theundefeated.com/features/during-world-war-ii-the-black-press-campaigned-for-a-double-victory-over-tyranny-abroad-and-segregation-at-home/

Harrington, Oliver. *Why I Left America and Other Essays.* Jackson: University Press of Mississippi, 1993.

Inge, M. Thomas. *Dark Laughter: The Satiric Art of Oliver W. Harrington.* Jackson: University Press of Mississippi, 1993.

Jackson, Tim. *Pioneering Cartoonists of Color.* (Jackson: University Press of Mississippi, 2016).

Smethurst, James and Rachel Rubin. "The Cartoons of Ollie Harrington, the Black Left, and the African American Press During the Jim Crow Era," *American Studies* 59.3 (Nov. 2020): 121-141.

Wanzo, Rebecca. *The Content of Our Caricature: African American Comic Art and Political Belonging.* (New York: NYU Press, 2020).

Washburn, Pat. "The *Pittsburgh Courier's* Double V Campaign in 1942," Paper presented at the Annual Meeting of the Association for Education in Journalism, Michigan State University, August 1981.

Wynn, Neil A. *The African American Experience during World War II.* Rowman & Littlefield Publishers, 2010.

ALSO AVAILABLE

BOOTSIE's BIG '50s

A DARK LAUGHTER COLLECTION BY OLLIE HARRINGTON

More than three years worth of gorgeous "Dark Laughter" panels from the 1950s in a nice, large format.

Comics that tell the tales of their times.

Vic the Vet

Cartoons about being a World War II vet going to college on the GI Bill... by a World War II vet as he was going to college on the GI Bill.

ISBN: 978-1-936404-65-0

Wasn't the Depression Terrible?

Cartoons about the Great Depression, drawn in 1934 by Reuben Award winner Otto Soglow, creator of The Little King.

ISBN: 978-1-949996-05-0

Ask for them where you got this book or head over to AboutComics.com

Not only does About Comics publish facsimile reprints of the classic travel guide for African Americans, the Green Book, we also offer the first-ever collection of Breezy - a comic strip by Green Book co-publisher and cover artist Mel Tapley (working as "Tap Melvin".)

www.ingramcontent.com/pod-product-compliance
Lightning Source LLC
Chambersburg PA
CBHW020021030726
47499CB00007B/2217